To Julie, Michael in Heaven, and Paul:
my children, my heart, my inspiration.

www.mascotbooks.com

The Hero of Hawk's Nest Beach: A Sea Turtle Rescue

For more information, please contact:
Mascot Books
620 Herndon Parkway, Suite 320
Herndon, VA 20170
info@mascotbooks.com

Library of Congress Control Number: 2021910406

CPSIA Code: PRT0721A
ISBN-13: 978-1-64543-329-3

Printed in the United States

The HERO of Hawk's Nest Beach

A Sea Turtle Rescue

Barbara Gervais Ciancimino

Illustrated by
Diana Delosh

It was a beautiful day on Long Island Sound. The water sparkled as the waves rushed ashore, leaving Lady Slipper shells along the edge of the sand. Off in the distance, the sound of children's laughter filled the air.

Finn and Little Mutt spent every summer together at Hawk's Nest Beach, chasing seagulls, playing with the children, and best of all, gobbling up the hot dogs that rolled off the grill.

Finn was a regular everyday dog, who didn't like being a regular everyday dog. He dreamed of being a fancy show dog like the ones on television. But today, he wasn't going to think about that. He was at the beach with Little Mutt and that made him happy.

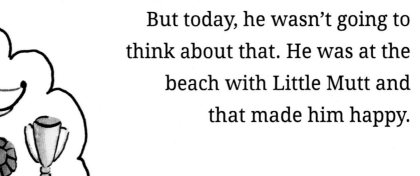

"Come on, Little Mutt," Finn called out.

"I'm coming," he answered.

Finn and Little Mutt were on a mission. They were headed to the rock jetty where the children were crabbing. As soon as they reached the rocks, they climbed to the top and headed to where everyone was gathered. They loved being around the children. There was always something fun happening wherever they were.

The moment Finn and Little Mutt reached the children, someone called out, "I caught one! Bring a bucket!" A little girl ran over with her pail, just as the crab was being raised out of the water. *PLOP!* Into the pail it dropped. Everyone gathered around to take a look. The crab, which was not too happy, leaned back on its swimming legs and raised its opened claws, startling the children.

The two dogs hurried over to see what all the fuss was about. Little Mutt went in for a closer look. That was not a good idea. The crab didn't like that he had come so close to him. It opened its pincers and tried to pinch him, right on the nose. Little Mutt tumbled backwards to get away from the crab, knocking the pail, crab and all, into the ocean. It slowly filled with water and sank. Everyone stood silent, except for the little girl, who began to cry...it was her pail.

Finn felt bad for the little girl, and without hesitating, jumped into the water.

Finn, who was good at finding things on the ocean floor, swam to the bottom. He searched in seaweed beds and behind rocks, but the pail was nowhere to be found. Then, just as he was about to give up, he noticed something moving at the bottom of a nearby boat piling.

As Finn swam closer, he could see a
fishing net wrapped around the piling,
and there, caught in the net, was a small
sea turtle...in big trouble. Its eyes were
wide with fear. Finn knew he had to work
fast. He took hold of the net and began
pulling and swimming around the post.

Finally, the net came free—but the turtle was still entwined. With no time to waste, Finn grabbed the net in his mouth and headed to shore with the sea turtle trailing behind.

A worried crowd had gathered on the beach waiting for Finn's return. Everyone cheered when they finally saw him come to the surface. They could see he was towing something behind him, so Little Mutt and the children ran into the water to help. They gasped in surprise when they saw the injured sea turtle tangled in the net.

Carefully, they carried the turtle onto the shore.
One of the dads phoned for help. "I'm calling the
aquarium," he said. "They'll know what to do."

Before long, a blue van drove onto the beach to where the people were gathered. Two volunteers from the Marine Animal Rescue jumped out of the vehicle and ran down to the turtle, carrying clippers and towels.

"Oh dear!" exclaimed one of the rescuers. "It's a Kemp's ridley sea turtle from the Gulf of Mexico. This is a rare and endangered species. You are far from home, little one," she said.

The two volunteers knelt and carefully cut the tangled net away from the turtle. Once the netting was removed, they wrapped its flippers and shell in wet towels and headed for the van.

While the volunteers were gone, Finn walked over to get a better look at the sea creature he had saved.

"Hello," he said. "I'm Finn."

The turtle looked up at him with a weak smile. "Hello, my name is Olive," she said. "Thank you for saving my life."

"You're welcome," whispered Finn.

Little Mutt walked over and stood beside him. "This is my best friend, Little Mutt," said Finn.

"He helped too."

"You are my heroes," said Olive.

When the rescuers returned, they lifted Olive
onto a stretcher and placed her into the van. The
two dogs watched as it drove out of sight. Sadly,
Finn and Little Mutt walked back to their cottages.
Neither one of them said a word.

Things were back to normal on Hawk's Nest Beach. Even the little girl's pail had washed up on shore several days later.

One afternoon, while Finn and Little Mutt were snoozing under a cottage, Finn heard a car coming up the beach. "Wake up," nudged Finn. "There's a car coming." The two dogs came out from under the house, just in time to see a blue van driving past them.

People had gathered around the van by the time Finn and Little Mutt reached it. Just as the two dogs made their way to the front of the crowd, the back doors opened. They couldn't believe their eyes. There was Olive, head held high, looking straight at them. She smiled, and raised her flipper to wave hello. Finn and Little Mutt were so happy to see her that they barked with joy and did a happy dog dance.

Then, hearing
one of the rescuers
begin to speak, everyone turned to listen.

"First," he began, "the sea turtle has made a full recovery and is ready to be released back into the ocean." Everyone cheered. "But, before we do, we would like to say thank you to the heroes who saved her."

"Finn and Little Mutt, please come forward," he said. "When you saw that the Kemp's ridley sea turtle was in danger, you did what you had to do to save her. You didn't think of yourself. You thought of her first. You are very special dogs."

A woman stepped forward with two bandanas. The dogs sat proudly as she tied them around their necks, making sure the picture of Olive was over their hearts.

Everyone watched as Olive was lifted off the stretcher and lowered onto the shore. "Go ahead little one," encouraged the rescuer. "Go home to the sea."

Olive pushed the sand with her flippers as she made her way to the water. When she reached the edge, she looked back and smiled at the two friends who had saved her life...then disappeared into the surf.

Finn and Little Mutt would never forget that day on Hawk's Nest Beach...the day they saved a sea turtle named Olive.

Finn had learned a lot about himself that summer. He realized that while the fancy show dogs on television were amazing, he was pretty amazing, too. He was kind-hearted and brave, and so grateful to have a friend like Little Mutt and a caring Forever Family, who loved him. Finn smiled...*I guess being a regular everyday dog isn't so bad after all,* he thought.

At long last, Finn had a happy heart.

20 FUN FACTS ABOUT KEMP'S RIDLEY SEA TURTLES

- The Kemp's ridley sea turtle is named after Richard M. Kemp, a fisherman and naturalist from Key West, Florida, who first saw the turtle in Florida and submitted it for identification in 1880.
- They are the rarest of all the sea turtles.
- They can be found in the Atlantic Ocean along the coast of the United States, from Florida to Maine, and as far north as Nova Scotia.
- The Kemp's ridley is the smallest of all the sea turtles, weighing between 75 and 100 pounds.
- They are 1½ inches long when they are born and grow to be about 30 inches long.
- They may live to be 50 years old.
- Their olive-gray upper shell, called a **carapace**, can be oval or heart-shaped.
- The turtles have front **flippers**, which are like hands without fingers. The front flippers have one claw and their back flippers have 1-2 claws.
  - Sea turtles are **reptiles**. They are cold-blooded, have scaly skin, breathe air through lungs, like we do, and lay eggs.
  - Kemp's ridley sea turtles can rest or sleep underwater for several hours at a time, but their underwater time is much shorter when they are diving for food or escaping trouble.

- The turtles **migrate** thousands of miles every year, moving from one place to another, looking for food.
- The Kemp's ridley sea turtles' favorite food is crab. They also eat jellyfish, clams, mussels, squid, and fish. They also like to munch on seaweed and algae.
- The sea turtles sleep on top of the water while out at sea or on the bottom, wedged under rocks, when they are close to shore.
- The female sea turtles travel hundreds of miles to reach their nesting beach.
- Thousands of female Kemp's ridley sea turtles return to the beach where they were hatched to make their nests and lay their eggs in a mass nesting called an **arribada (air-a-bod-o)**, a Spanish word meaning "arrival by sea."
- They make their nests from May to July, and unlike any other sea turtles, they lay their eggs during the daylight hours.
- The female turtles use their flippers to dig an **egg chamber**, a hole in the sand where they lay their eggs.
- They typically lay 100 eggs that hatch in 50 to 55 days. The baby sea turtles then crawl into the ocean and swim out to sea.
- The Kemp's ridley is the most endangered of all the sea turtles.
- They are in danger from shrimp nets, eating floating trash that they think is food, and changes in their **habitat**, the place where they live and grow.

ABOUT THE AUTHOR

Barbara is a retired elementary school teacher who lives in New England with her husband, Jim, and their dog, Ty. Together, they have five children and ten grandchildren, who are the inspiration for her writing. She was born and raised in the city of Hartford, Connecticut, where she later spent twenty-four years teaching reading, writing, and science to grades three through eight. Still a teacher at heart, Barbara enjoys incorporating scientific facts about her characters into her stories.

Barbara graduated magna cum laude from Central Connecticut State University with a master's degree in elementary education. She has been a member of the Society of Children's Book Writers and Illustrators since 2015 and a member of the Connecticut Authors and Publishers Association since 2018. She is also the author of an award-winning children's picture book entitled *Odonata: The Flying Jewel of Maiden Grass Pond*, which won a Mom's Choice Award (Gold Award Recipient), the Story Monsters Approved for School Life Award, and the Purple Dragonfly Book Award for School Issues.

One of Barbara's talents is baking and creating character and wedding cakes for family and friends. She also loves spending time at the beach with her family and having adventures with her grandchildren.